THE RIVER PHOENIX ALBUM

PENELOPE DENING

THUNDER'S
MOUTH
PRESS

First Thunder's Mouth Press edition, 1996

Published by
Thunder's Mouth Press
632 Broadway, 7th Floor
New York, NY 10012

First published in Great Britain in 1995
by Plexus Publishing Limited, London
This edition published by arrangement
with Plexus Publishing Limited

Dening, Penelope
The River Phoenix Album/Penelope Dening
  1. River Phoenix   2. Motion Picture Actors - American -
  Photographs
  ISBN 1-56025-130-1
  Library of Congress Cataloguing Number: 96-60032

Cover and book design by Phil Smee
Printed in Spain by Graficas Reunidas SA

Acknowledgements

The Publishers would like to thank the following newspapers and magazines for
their assistance in research: *The Daily Express, Empire, The Evening Standard,
Gay Times, The Guardian, The Independent on Sunday, Interview Magazine,
Just Seventeen, The Los Angeles Times, The Mail on Sunday, The Modern Review,
The Monthly Film Bulletin, The National Enquirer, New York Magazine, The New
York Star, The New York Times, People Weekly, Premiere (UK), Premiere (US),
Select, Sight and Sound, Sky Magazine, The Spectator, Spin, The Sun, The Times,
TV Guide, Variety, The Village Voice, The Washington Post.*
    The Publishers would also like to thank the following for supplying photographs:
All Action Pictures; British Film Institute; Lance Staedler/Katz/Botaish Group;
Diego Uchitel/Katz/Outline; Peggy Sirota/Katz/Outline; Stephen Ellison/Katz;
Michael Tighe/Katz/Outline; Nancy Rica Schiff/Katz/Saga Agency; Lance Staedler/
Retna/Onyx; Nancy Ellison/ Retna/Onyx; Robert Matheu/Retna; Timothy White/
Retna/Onyx; Bonnie Schiffman/Retna; Rob Brown/ Retna; Stephen Ellison/
Scope/Shooting Star; Nancy Ellison/Sygma; John Huba/Sygma; G. Rose/
Frank Spooner/Gamma Liaison.

'The main thing in film acting is something going on in the face. And with the really good ones, it's pain. You don't read it as pain, but when you look, it's pain.'

Gus van Sant
Director, My Own Private Idaho

FADE IN

EXT: SUNSET STRIP, WEST HOLLYWOOD SIDEWALK : NIGHT
FOUR FANCY-DRESSED REVELLERS wander through a cornucopia of neon: a green-faced WITCH, a wannabe LOUIS XIV FOP, a white-faced HARLEQUIN and THE GRIM REAPER, complete with scythe. In front of them a BLACK DERELICT lurches from doorway to darkened doorway. With camp precision the FOP steps over protruding legs and we see the slumped body of DRUNK. Welcome to Hallowe'en Hollywood style. THE GRIM REAPER accosts a STRAIGHT-LOOKING WHITE COUPLE as they hail a cab.

                    GRIM REAPER:
                    Trick or treat?

THE REVELLERS laugh as the flustered COUPLE escape into the cab before they join the throng in front of the black-canopied entrance to 'The Viper Room', latest addition to the Strip's Nite Spots. ED, THE BLACK BOUNCER, built like Fort Knox, surveys the REVELLERS through wraparound black sunglasses. The REVELLERS cavort for his benefit but he takes no notice.

The REVELLERS' path down Sunset is suddenly blocked as the stage door to 'The Viper Room' crashes open to reveal LEAF and SAMANTHA carrying convulsing body of unconscious RIVER, followed by distraught RAIN. Rock Music (THE RED HOT CHILLI PEPPERS) pounds from inside. Panic surrounds them. LEAF and SAMANTHA unload the heavy body of RIVER onto the edge of the sidewalk, his head towards the gutter. RAIN kneels next to him. She pulls up his shirt, rubs his stomach and shouts, desperate to wake up her twitching yet unconscious brother.

> RAIN:
> Can you hear me?
> Can you hear me?

THE REVELLERS watch the sidewalk side-show. RIVER has the first of five fits. He's dressed in black jeans, black shirt and white-laced Converse trainers. His body is convulsing. His head hits the sidewalk. His young face is ghostly pale. His eyes roll up and disappear under twitching eyelids. His short dark hair is matted from vomit. His shirt is wet where vomit has been inexpertly wiped. His clenched knuckles pound the sidewalk.

CUT TO: THE UNSHOCKABLE REVELLERS
THE WITCH and HARLEQUIN pass a joint between them. THE GRIM REAPER cleans his nails with the end of his scythe. Behind them ED continues to check in guests. Behind them we hear the raised voice of SAMANTHA as she tries to get ED's attention.

> SAMANTHA:
> Do something – Do something. Call 911.
> Just do something can't you?

ED is unconcerned and continues to check in guests.

THE GRIM REAPER motions to the other REVELLERS to follow. He's had enough of the side-show. As they move up the sidewalk THE GRIM REAPER is forced to step over RIVER'S flailing body.

> WITCH:
> Urgh. How gross.

A few PEOPLE have started to gather: some SHARP DRESSERS have been drawn from the 'Whisky A Go Go' across the street, some YOUNGER DUDES and GRUNGE BABES on their way to 'The Viper Room'. All watch impassively as RAIN now lies on top of RIVER trying to quell his thrashing body. The Hollywood Hip have no idea that this is RIVER PHOENIX, one of Hollywood's million-dollar earners, icon to a generation, their generation. But the boy with short brown hair and raddled face bears no resemblance to the floppy-haired teen dream they grew up with at the movies. To the watchers it's just another junkie. Just another show.

                              RAIN:
                              (to anyone who will listen)
                              Get an ambulance, won't you. Please,
                              someone just get an ambulance.

A GIRL, one of the more sober from among the spaced out ENTOURAGE who have drifted out through the Stage Door of 'The Viper Room', puts her finger into RIVER'S mouth to try and stop him from swallowing his tongue. A YOUNG MAN is splashing him with water from a beer glass.

CUT TO: EXT. TELEPHONE BOOTH
LEAF, RIVER'S younger brother is talking to the emergency services. He is in tears. His speech is muffled. He is utterly distraught, his eyes turning toward the sidewalk. Sometimes he sounds threatening, sometimes apologetic.

CUT TO: INT. TELEPHONE BOOTH

                              LEAF:
                              I don't know.
                              I'm thinking he had Valium or something.

CUT TO: EXT. SIDEWALK

The CROWD have moved back. Although an Ambulance pulls up a few yards off they are still not that concerned. On the sidewalk Emergency Medical Equipment surrounds RIVER. A PARAMEDIC kneels at the side of the now inert body. He rips away RIVER'S shirt and begins to pump his chest. Another PARAMEDIC injects him with resuscitating drugs. But it's too late.

As RIVER is carried into the waiting ambulance in a stretcher FLEA, bassist with THE RED HOT CHILLI PEPPERS, emerges from the stage door, having just heard the news.

> FLEA:
> (screaming)
> I'm going with him.

FLEA tries to jump into the back but is directed to get in the front of the ambulance. As the ambulance pulls away we see SAMANTHA and RAIN standing motionless on the sidewalk. Behind them LEAF is banging his head against the wall.

CUT TO INT. AMBULANCE and RIVER'S MASK-LIKE FACE

FADE OUT

ROLL TITLES:

RIVER PHOENIX:

THE REBEL WITH TOO MANY CAUSES

' When I first met River, he had very long
hair and he struck me – as he came out of
an elevator – as an angel, some kind of
supernatural being. An angel could be
Gabriel, but an angel could be Lucifer too.
He could as readily delve in to the deep,
dark recesses as he would fly up to
the lofty, illuminated [places]. '

Bobby Bukowski,
Director of Photography, Dogfight

It was always tempting to read parallels between the life River Phoenix lived off-screen
and the roles he played on film. Were his mesmerising performances the rare meshing of
talent and technique? Or were they just the result of exploitative casting? And did the
blurring of fact and fiction, vehemently denied by Phoenix himself, lead to the death
only a Hollywood screenwriter could have penned?

How otherwise could the clean-living, green-thinking, all-American blue-eyed boy
whose unblemished skin and firm body made a mockery of those who said that only
meat can make a man of you, come to die in a Hollywood gutter?

According to the coroner's report, River Phoenix died of an overdose of drugs. But
Jim Barton, screenwriter of *Dark Blood*, the film River was within days of finishing, has
a darker, angrier view: 'River Phoenix was a victim of the machine. The fame machine,
the Hollywood machine, the selling machine, the money machine. And the machine is a
liar.'

Hollywood is an industry. It deals in product. Talent, looks, personalities and personal
histories are all part of the package, there to be marketed, there to be exploited. A
history of victimhood, of child abuse? Just so long as it wasn't your fault. From Marilyn
Monroe to Carrie Fisher, it's nothing new. Keep it simple. And stay clean. No
communists, homosexuals or unusual sexual appetites allowed. No drunks, no junkies.
It doesn't help to alienate the public or the studio heads.

The best myths, like the best lies, are based on truth. But if the parasite of myth is
allowed to flourish unchecked, its host, the truth, eventually disappears. For River
Phoenix that truth was his identity. Its loss resulted in his death. As a myth-making
machine, Hollywood is unsurpassed. It pumps up the good and silences the bad. The
currency here is happy endings. Never mind reality feel the myth. As Jim Barton
explained: 'In Hollywood censorship is so total it's invisible. It's a wonder anyone

survives, surrounded by fawning fans, agents and image makers telling them they're the most wonderful thing around; paid a million dollars for eight weeks' work, given everything they want, whenever they want. If you're a star in Hollywood you only go to the bathroom yourself because it's physically impossible for somebody else to offer to do it for you.'

The antidote to this poison is regular doses of the truth – home truths – from parents, siblings, long term lovers, whose love is real, strong and fearless. The tragedy for River Phoenix was that his family were major investors in the myth-making business themselves.

The image of River as eco-saviour to the planet was no two-in-the-morning creative blast from a Hollywood spin doctor. It was conceived and nurtured by River's own parents whose caring, sharing eco-life was a sad parody of the postwar generation's search for a value system that would hold. Both were in flight from backgrounds they were (and still are) hell bent on denying. River's mother Arlyn Dunetz was born in 1944 into a conventional Jewish family from the Bronx. One of three sisters, Arlyn was no high flier and after leaving High School worked as a secretary in Manhattan where she met and married a computer programmer. For reasons that remain unknown (though with the benefit of hindsight she claims it was her awareness of pollution), at 22 Arlyn saw the light: 'I became aware. It was difficult because my parents weren't seeing the same things, but I knew. I had to change my life.'

Interestingly, this post-facto reminiscence makes no reference to her abandoned husband. The myth-making machine had started to roll. Arlyn headed West, hitch-hiking to California with a friend. But her decision to make for the glitz of Hollywood rather than the kaftans of San Francisco suggests that the changes she sought were weighted on the side of fame and fortune rather than the intellectual freedom and spiritual

THE
RIVER
PHOENIX
ALBUM

enlightenment she claims.

Appropriately enough it was in Hollywood, on Santa Monica Boulevard, that Arlyn Dunetz met her fate. The scenario of the meeting of Arlyn and John is classic road-movie stuff. Girl hitches lift from Boy in battered Volkswagen van and never looks back. They drink, they smoke. Love at first vibration. John was tall, stooping and bearded. According to legend he was a High School dropout. By night he wrote poetry and strummed his guitar. By day, more prosaically – as even hippies needed to eat and fill their trucks with gas – he restored furniture.

For a year John and Arlyn hit the hippy trail, moving around the western states. Rejection of the Vietnam war – and by extension the society that had spawned it – had made such rag-tag travellers commonplace anywhere a few dollars could be made and no questions asked. They called themselves 'seekers'. Seekers after enlightenment. But until they found the real thing, LSD would do.

By early 1970 Arlyn was pregnant and that summer the couple headed north, joining a fellow band of travellers seeking an unfettered life in Madras, Oregon, peppermint capital of the world. Like Arlyn, John too was escaping from a past. John's background was far from stable. He was a native Californian, from Fontana, a steel town fifty miles east of Los Angeles. But life in Fontana had more in common with the urban misery of Springsteen's New Jersey than the Beachboy's Surfin USA. Not for nothing was it the birthplace of Hells Angels. All anyone wanted to do in Fontana was to get out. A car crash left John's mother irreversibly brain damaged. His father upped and left, eventually to remarry and settle in Perth, Australia. At thirteen John ran away 'to Hollywood', was eventually found and returned to the care of his aunt Frances. Early profiles tell of a history of 'juvenile homes and drink problems'. This has never been confirmed, though problems with drink – particularly when away from Arlyn's whip hand – would haunt

his relationship with River right till the end. When asked to expand on this, or any other less appealing aspect of their early lives, Arlyn's answer would be 'It is part of the past and no longer relevant.' Also no longer relevant was John's previous marriage and daughter. But his denial of his past is most forcefully illustrated in the rejection of his own name.

To John and Arlyn, a rose by any other name did not smell as sweet. According to Roy Nance, the young farmer who employed them to hoe his fields of peppermint and from whom they rented the house outside Madras, Oregon where their first child would be born, John's surname was Bottom. In American-English the name is not as pejorative as it is in English-English. (It presented no barriers to the American actor Timothy Bottoms.) But for John names were talismanic, with magical properties for good or evil. His own name was proof. Bottom he had been called, so to the bottom he had sunk. But banks are disinclined to deal in anonymity, so the young farmer who paid out the wages made the cheque out to John's full name. To Nance the name only seemed worthy of comment when he heard what his young tenants had called their baby. As he later explained, 'River Bottom sure ain't the kind of name you hear in Madras.'

The names John and Arlyn gave to their children were all imbued with symbolic significance, runes to empower the bearer with the qualities enshrined in the word itself. John's abandoned daughter had been bequeathed the sadly inappropriate name of Trust. River was from the River of Life, taken from Herman Hesse's mystical novel *Siddhartha* that was enjoying a new lease of cult life in the mid-sixties. River was to be the incarnate realisation of all their ideals. But like many of their ideals their thinking was incomplete and half-baked, though in this case tragically prophetic. A river feeds the land and those around it; its path is shaped by external forces. It has no independent

life but is simply a channel and it carries its burden without choice. As a family friend later remarked: 'River was going to change the world. He was their new dawn. And that is a hell of a lot for any kid to handle.'

Although professionally his name never did River Phoenix any harm, psychologically it was a burden he could have done without. Not only were there the weighty metaphysical implications – which he was never allowed to forget, either by his family or the media – but children are by nature conformists and River was to suffer the usual run of taunts and feeble puns which are the lot of anyone saddled with an unconventional name. With every move (and it is claimed they had forty homes in twenty years) and with every film, he'd find himself yet again the butt of the same tired jokes. Later in his teens he confessed that he would 'have preferred a name that blended in more with my surroundings'. Like Scott or Steve, he said. But, as ever, his anxiety not to be seen to criticise his parents shines through and he continued with eighteen-year-old disingenuousness: 'But now I've really learned to love it. From fifteen I really liked it, it felt appropriate. Before then I don't think it quite fitted me. I had to grow into it.'

River's second name would also be sadly apt, although its significance was undoubtedly unknown to John and Arlyn at the time. As far as they were aware Jude came from 'Hey Jude', the Beatles' hit of the year of his birth. But if his parents' reading had extended beyond cult novels to the work of Thomas Hardy, they would have known that Jude is the patron saint of lost causes.

River Phoenix was born as he lived and as he died. In public. Not for him the intimate awakening that is the birthright of us all, but a public performance. This time the central role was taken by his mother, surrounded by a cast of well-wishers who, she would later recount, 'roared with approval' when the baby took its first gulp of air. Rites of passage are important to everyone and none more so, as far as River's parents were concerned,

than for their firstborn. And the myth-making machinery was already at work. The rustic 'log-cabin' of his birth was in reality a four-bedroom house which they shared with fellow travellers. The natural birth with not a medic in sight was also wishful thinking. True, they had not asked for a doctor, but their landlord Roy Nance had made sure the local midwife was on hand when the time came just the same.

But the final gloss on River's nativity was withheld until after his death. In the blaze of grim publicity surrounding the Hollywood Memorial service, Arlyn (by now modestly renamed Heart) reviewed his birth. The labour, she told mourners, was arduous in the extreme. By the time River was born it had lasted three and a half days. The explanation for this had been made clear to her in a vision: 'River didn't want to be in the world.' It had been up to God to convince River that the world needed him. For, as River had explained to God, 'I'd rather stay up here with you.' So God and River-to-be bargained, Arlyn said. Eventually God's entreaties won, and a deal was struck. At first River would only agree to spending five years on earth, then he upped it to ten. Finally they shook hands on 23. Only then did he agree to be born. Hence the delay.

Truth, as John and Arlyn soon learnt, was what you wanted it to be. Like anything else that was marketable, it could be pruned and teased to increase its appeal.

John, Arlyn and baby River stayed in Oregon till early winter and then the Volkswagen train moved south seeking the sun and enlightenment. They did not have to wait long. For St Paul it was the road to Damascus. For John and Arlyn it would be Pike's Peak, Colorado.

In the sixties the post-war generation had come of age. The axis of capitalist and Christian beliefs that had sustained America for three hundred years had tilted. The assassinations of John and Robert Kennedy and of Martin Luther King had rocked any

sense that Uncle Sam was in control. The war in Vietnam had robbed young Americans not only of their friends but of their sense of belonging. Disaffected from the flag and everything it represented, yet nurtured in a community of rigid values, what they were seeking was not so much enlightenment as a replacement set of beliefs and a new family. They needed to belong.

Flower power itself was based on a woolly idea of eastern mysticism and had its genesis in the Beatles' discovery of transcendental meditation through the Maharishi Mahesh Yogi. By the seventies the Hare Krishnas with their incongruously shaven heads, yellow robes and begging bowls were a familiar sight in shopping malls from Frankfurt to Chicago. Incongruous they might have been. Innocuous they were not. The tawdry story of the Hare Krishnas includes drug-running, prostitution and murder, and many of the religious cults which mushroomed simultaneously were similarly suspect. The horror stories of the Jonestown Massacre and David Koresh's Waco apocalypse are only the tip of the iceberg, as can be seen from the Aum gas attack on the Tokyo underground in the Spring of 1995.

Cults are about power: wielding it and submitting to it. They attract, and feed on, the socially and emotionally dysfunctional. In Pike's Peak, Colorado, John and Arlyn were easy pickings for the sect known as the Children of God. This cult derived its energy from one Messiah-like man, David Berg, known as Moses David. Like all cult-leaders Berg was a megalomaniac. His omniscience and thus his power was total.

Any and every kind of power perversion can break out in this climate, and as history has shown, usually does. The Children of God were no exception. The system worked a little like pyramid selling. What was on sale was love. To prove your faith and submission to the leader, to be worthy of his love, you had to recruit. The Children of God were not alone in using amorally-structured fund-raising activities. Sex was regularly used both to

ensnare converts and by those higher up the pyramid to exert power through humiliation. It only took a twist of focus and language for indiscriminate sex to be sold as unconditional love. The more converts you made, the higher you would rise in the hierarchy, submissive to those above you, aggressive to those below. Clothed in the vestments of 'have-a-nice-day' spiritual superiority, the Children of God conferred identity and status to those who belonged, with the full panoply of spurious religious edicts derived from selective misinterpretations of the Bible or other quasi-religious texts.

Later John and Arlyn would describe themselves as 'missionaries'. Their mission was simply to recruit new converts. Working as ever among the dispossessed and vulnerable they made their way south. Their first documented stop was Crockett, Texas where a sister for River, Rain Joan of Arc, was born in 1973. Next they pushed on to Mexico and Puerto Rico, where their second son Joaquin (Spanish for John) was born. (At four he changed his name to Leaf, not wanting to be the only one of the children without a 'nature' name. At sixteen he changed it back again.)

By 1975 their roll-call of converts was impressive enough to warrant John's official designation as Archbishop to South America, and child number four, Libertad Mariposa (Liberty Butterfly) was born in Caracas, Venezuela. 'Missionary' work was not only limited to John and Arlyn however. Although River and Rain were only five and two they were already drop-dead cute. In the early seventies Venezuela was booming and the streets of Caracas were running with petro dollars. Who could resist handing over their loose change (or something bigger and better) to these innocent kids, singing negro spirituals outside their smart Caracas hotels or tap dancing in the airport, collecting money and handing out pamphlets.

'Moses' David Berg knew the value of children. The sexual seduction of potential

converts by the women of the sect was a standard technique, and known as 'flirty fishing'. Nuns call themselves Brides of Christ; these women were happily referred to as 'hookers for Jesus'. But the sexual freedoms advocated by Berg's cult went further than that. In 1993, 69 members of The Children of God were arrested in Argentina and charged with various crimes relating to incest and paedophilia. Whether River or his brother or sisters were ever used as sexual honeypots or experienced any kind of sexual molestation themselves is not known. In interviews later in life River would claim to have lost his virginity at the age of four. But at other times he would deny the claim, saying that it was just a joke. But, even if they were not directly abused, they were brought up in an atmosphere in which the exploitation of children was permitted and accepted.

River Phoenix was six when John and Arlyn eventually saw the light. He would never be drawn on his experiences of those days beyond vehemently disowning the cult. Indeed, seeking mitigation for his parents he would naively claim they had got involved 'not out of choice but more like a desperate situation'. But according to people he later worked with, River often showed what they felt was an 'unhealthy' interest in the nature of prostitution, particularly in the role of the pimp.

As far as Arlyn is concerned, she and John knew nothing of the cult's seamy side until 1976 and their response when they discovered the true nature of what was going on was one of shock and revulsion. Yet it is hard to believe that they knew as little as they claim about what was going on, given John's rise to the heights of Archbishop. Neither of them has ever expressed any regret about the part they had played or the time they had spent in the organisation: from their stand-point the Children of God had given their lives a breadth and purpose far beyond anything they could have achieved without it. Years later, even after River's death, John still could not entirely disown his mentor

David Berg: 'It took us five years to realise that they were wrong. He may have been a sexual pervert but he is still a better man than a lot of people.'

Once again the family found themselves adrift without a support system. They had four children, three under five, and according to myth they were destitute and living in a vermin-infested beach-shack on the Venezuelan cost. River and Rain's song and dance act was now central to the family's survival. Later River would make light of it, another sad justification of the path his parents had chosen for him. 'It was a great stepping stone. I learned to play the guitar there – my sister Rain and I got interested in performing. It was a neat time to be growing up in Venezuela in the late seventies.'

Arlyn, now pregnant with her fifth and last child (another daughter, Summer Joy, born in Florida), had had enough. At least in America there would be welfare, if not work. According to River, the family was eventually helped to stow away. 'A priest got us on this old Tonka freighter that carried Tonka toys. We were stowaways. The crew discovered us half way home – and threw a big birthday party for my brother, and we got all these damaged Tonka toys. It was a blast.'

It was probably on this trip, when Leaf saw the sailors killing fish by banging their heads against the hull of the boat, that the family became vegans. Claims that they had always been vegan are probably untrue. When you're down and out in South America you eat what you can get. And what is generally available on the streets of Caracas is not tofu burgers.

But returning to America was not to be seen a retreat. From the ashes of the Children of God the family would be reborn. As proof, they adopted the symbolically loaded name of Phoenix – the mythological bird who rises from the ashes. Once again they could have researched the myth more thoroughly. The phoenix sets itself on fire just to re-live the same life over again.

Moses David might have failed to lead them into the promised land but evangelism was now in their blood. All that was needed was a new crusade and what better than the environment, with veganism their calling card. Nothing that had anything to do with animals could be countenanced. No milk or dairy products. No honey. No leather shoes.

In 1977, they moved in with Arlyn's parents who had retired to Winter Park, a suburb of Orlando, Florida. With such a young family Arlyn had her hands full and so John returned to his old skills, working as a carpenter and as a gardener. But within months of their return disaster struck. When the last baby Summer Joy was only three months old her father injured his back. His days as breadwinner were over. In Caracas they'd been bailed out by the children's singing and dancing. Why not here? To those who questioned Arlyn's decision to risk the hell of Hollywood she replied, 'It is only right to allow River and his brother and sisters to express their natural talent.' But after River's death, and after his split with Arlyn, John Phoenix was to belie the myth: 'The original idea was to milk the system and to be financially secure.'

Although John would continue to act as River's chaperon throughout his career, as required by law, his response to 'the new Babylon' as he would later call it, was at best ambivalent. Whether this stemmed simply from the shame of having his role usurped by his son, or whether from a real fear of the nature of Hollywood (his own reading) will never be known. But right from the outset there was never any question that however much 'we' was used, the driving force behind River's career was Arlyn. Eventually it drove the couple apart and about a year before River's death John returned to a sub-hippy existence in Costa Rica, where he now lives alone.

God might have abandoned them momentarily in Venezuela but he had certainly made up for it now. The young Phoenix's won talent show after talent show. The final spring board was the Hernando Fiesta where their performance merited rave reviews in

the local press and was seen by a well-to-do young man called Sky Sworski who was so impressed he became the family's devoted advisor and benefactor. They were cute and nimble of foot. They could sing, tap dance and play guitar. What else could America want? Arlyn was once more a woman with a mission: 'We had a vision that our kids could captivate the world.'

River, not unnaturally, was captivated by the very idea of movies and television. For a boy bought up barefoot in South America it must have been the apotheosis of everything this new life had to offer: 'I became instantly fascinated by the mysteries of film making and I was desperate to get involved. I wondered how it could be so real when it was actually just a bunch of actors performing.'

Fuelled by his mother's fervour, River never had any doubt that he would make it, although he imagined that it would be through music, which would always remain his first and last love. ('I thought we would become the next Jackson Five!') After five years with the Children of God, Arlyn had all the techniques of persuasion at her disposal. It was just a question of when.

' People are constantly trying to make an image for you. They'll dress you up and tell you to pose a certain way and take all these pictures. . . they want a certain image, so they create that. And unless you're spending a lot of time to create another image to counteract that image, theirs will win. So right now, I'm kind of dealing with a lot of false ideas of what I'm about. '

River Phoenix

On 25th November 1993 a Memorial Service was held for River Phoenix at Paramount Studios, the oldest surviving studio in Hollywood. Built in 1917, Paramount backs onto the Hollywood Memorial Cemetery, final resting place of the first Hollywood heart throb Rudolf Valentino, whose death caused a nation to mourn and several young women to commit suicide. The venue was appropriate. It was a letter from the Head of Talent at Paramount that had given the Phoenix family the green light to leave Florida behind and head west for the big time and Hollywood. And, after a couple of years of commercials, musical variety spots with Rain and TV bit parts, it was with Paramount that River made his feature film debut in 1985 with *Explorers*. It had taken four years.

Holding Arlyn's hand in support at the Hollywood Memorial was Rob Reiner, director of *Stand By Me* (1986), River's second feature film and the one in which his compelling old-before-his-time sense of responsibility hinted at a lifetime of unspoken pain. This was the first indication that River Phoenix had talent that would outpace his peers. Past experience and unexpressed griefs provide fertile material for all actors. It is because child actors rarely have that kind of emotional baggage to bring into play, that their performances rarely extend beyond the cute and one-dimensional. But in River Phoenix, Rob Reiner recognised a lack of self-esteem unusual in nascent Hollywood stars: 'I did get the sense that he was searching and confused about things, and insecure... He didn't have a lot of technique – you just saw this kind of raw naturalism. You just turned the camera on, and he would tell the truth.'

From first to last, River acted with a reckless entirety. This would reach its apogee in *My Own Private Idaho* (1991) where the role of a narcoleptic, drug-happy rent boy would draw him into a dark world from which, ultimately, he was unable to escape.

But even from the start, it was River Phoenix's performance that lifted Rob Reiner's low-budget *Stand By Me* to a cult and box-office hit. It is hardly surprising that Peter

Weir, whose own films have regularly crossed the low-budget/cult divide, was tempted by River when he started to cast *The Mosquito Coast* (1986). As Weir said: 'He has the look of someone who has secrets.' Set in the jungles of central America, the film is narrated by young Charlie Fox who ultimately becomes the family's saviour. With its uncanny echoes of the Phoenix family's own history, Weir rightly believed that River's 'missionary' past could only add to his portrayal of the boy uprooted with the rest of the family by an obsessional father, to carve out a new life in the rain forest. Charlie's relationship with his father is riven with emotional tension, as he both idolises and resents the inventor-genius.

While Harrison Ford, River's on-screen father, built up a warm and mutually satisfying relationship with River, the relationship of son and blood-father, on location as chaperon, was rather closer to the one in the script and fraught with difficulties. Chaperon to River had over the years in Hollywood become John Phoenix's only money-making role. Peter Weir was well aware of the difficulties and articulated this dilemma: 'With a young person who suddenly becomes the key breadwinner of a family there's an incredible amount of rearranging of hierarchy, and at times a tension develops, particularly with the father. River wanted to compensate. He didn't want to spoil the family's closeness.' So father and son would sit and write songs together, but to outsiders it always seemed forced. Although it was clear to everyone that John had a drink problem, River was constantly coming to his father's defence and praising him. Later, Suzanne Solgot, River's girlfriend around the time he made *Idaho*, remembered how hard River tried to get close to his father: 'River would drink with his dad, so they could relate. But he worried the disease [alcoholism] was in his bloodline.'

Martha Plimpton saw the relationship at close quarters as both River's on-screen co-star and off-screen girlfriend in *The Mosquito Coast* and *Running On Empty* (1988).

She was one of the few people River was able to confide in: 'We had five million talks about his compulsive personality and his guilt and fear over not being able to save his father.' But River never gave up trying to reach his father and at the time of his death was planning to direct a film about John's abuse-punctuated childhood called *By Way Of Fontana*, which would star Leaf (Joaquin) as the young John Bottom.

Yet River was only sixteen when *The Mosquito Coast* was being shot: the age when rebelling against your family is a rite of passage central to emergence as an independent adult. In River's case, the standard avenues for rebellion were lined with danger. But whenever his father was not around he would rebel, pigging out on Mars Bars and Diet Coke, quite unabashed the next day about remonstrating with others for having the temerity to drink Coke in his presence. Interviewers would be chided for their non-P.C. behaviour, from cigarette-smoking to hamburger-eating. Yet everyone knew that River Phoenix smoked. But they also knew it wasn't to be acknowledged and he tried to ensure he was never photographed with a cigarette in his hand. Nobody minded this innocent discrepancy. ('I don't want to disillusion my fans', he said.) River Phoenix was a welcome alternative to the other nihilistic brat packers of his generation. And who could blame him, as somebody said, if all you were allowed to eat was birdfood.

In *Stand By Me*, River Phoenix was still a child actor. In *The Mosquito Coast*, his potential as brooding romantic was clear for all to see. To capitalise on this, his next outing was the teen comedy *A Night In The Life Of Jimmy Reardon* (1988). River himself saw it as 'a vehicle that could take me out of the boy thing. I figured it could help me to grow up. It wasn't meant to be a teenage film.' If helping him grow up meant confronting his parents and winning, it was a success. The story of the sexually-experienced junior Casanova did not go down well with John Phoenix. But once again Arlyn had the casting vote.

Teen dream though he undoubtedly was, the mantle of hard-bitten womaniser didn't really fit and by common consent *A Night In The Life of Jimmy Reardon* is a mess – neither teen flick, morality tale nor Graduate-style comedy. The director of the film, William Richert, was himself the original for the character of Jimmy Reardon. For the first time neither John nor Arlyn were present as chaperons on the set, leaving a powerful vacuum in which star and director were to forge a relationship that would last right through till River's death.

The search for a father-figure, with values River recognised and could respond to, would continue throughout his life. And the relationships appear to have been reciprocated. Harrison Ford was the first. Later there was Richard Harris in *Silent Tongue* (1993): 'He looked on me as a father figure. He'd knock on my door and ask if he could sleep.' Alan Bates, also in *Silent Tongue*: 'He was hugely fond of my son. My other son and my wife died and River was wonderful to my surviving son. He talked to him for hours over the phone when his mother died. I think River was like my late son. He was years ahead of his age. I think people like that are very vulnerable to... well, to other people. They are prey for the not-so-good.' Jonathan Pryce, co-star on *Dark Blood* (1993), River's last and unfinished film, said after River's death: 'What was so painful about it was the future relationship that I looked forward to. I felt it was a relationship that would go on for a long time. I wanted my children to know him and him to know them.'

There is no doubt that River's wholesale identification with his roles was magnified by the already existing parallels between his on- and off-screen lives. Casting to type is standard Hollywood procedure, often with good reason. With most screen actors, what you see is what you get. There is no more. *A Night In The Life of Jimmy Reardon* would be the aberration that proved the rule. After *The Mosquito Coast* the mould was set: boy

struggles with discovery that parents are not infallible: takes responsibility: grows up. And River's next two films would share this basic theme but in entirely different ways.

In *Little Nikita* (1988), all-American boy (Jeff) discovers that Mom and Pop are Russian spies, goes ape, comes to terms with it – and they all live happily ever after. The on-screen father-son relationship in *Little Nikita* is not with Jeff's real father but with the FBI agent on their tail, who is played by Sidney Poitier, one of the few black actors whom white audiences would accept in such a delicate bonding role. Once again, however, the film was a mess: cold war thriller scuppered by Boys' Own plot. Given the ludicrous storyline, however, River acquitted himself well.

But with *Running On Empty*, River Phoenix returned to surer territory. Once again the parallels with his own life are obvious: hippy parents (this time political activists in the 1960s) on the run from society (the FBI) since eldest son Danny was two. Now Danny's turned seventeen and has the chance of a life of his own as a talented pianist. But the Feds are closing in and the parents must move on. Danny finds the strength this time to take his chance alone. Fuelled by River's personal, if unconscious, struggle to escape his parents' hold on his career, there is an emotional dynamo in River's performance that in turn gives the whole film its high-voltage charge.

River Phoenix was nominated for an Academy Award for Best Supporting Actor in *Running On Empty*. He may have lost out (to Kevin Kline in *A Fish Called Wanda*) but an Oscar nomination showed he was now in the big league. As if in acknowledgement of that, his next role would be in a sure-fire blockbuster, playing the young Indiana in *Indiana Jones and the Last Crusade* (1989). Although they didn't get to act together on screen, Harrison Ford's admiration for the boy who played his son in *The Mosquito Coast* was thoroughly vindicated. At the news of River's death, he said he had been 'proud to watch him grow into a man of such talent, integrity and passion'.

By the time River made *Indiana Jones* he was the prime source of income for the whole Phoenix family. But he was never the decision-maker. Until *Indiana Jones and the Last Crusade*, when the decision was made to buy a property back in Florida, the Phoenix family had been permanently on the move, renting here and there, never staying anywhere more than a few months. Privacy in the conventional sense of having your own bedroom, having private relationships with siblings or parents, was unknown to River Phoenix. Even in the Florida property the Phoenix children shared bedrooms, and while it wasn't long before River moved out, renting his own place in nearby Gainesville, he was still well within the Phoenix family orbit. Within the ethos of the Children of God, privacy allowed for thought and shared unease. Secrets were dangerous, and this view was carried through into the Phoenix family's life back in America. Yet the early practice of hiding the truth beneath a well-constructed myth became second nature to River. As an actor, it gave him enormous power, as a man it destroyed him.

Naomi Foner, screenwriter of *Running On Empty*, believes that River Phoenix's extreme immersion in the characters he played was simply that he had no other way. He was, she said, 'totally, totally uneducated'. When he acted, she explained, 'he wasn't thinking about anything. Some of the reason he was so talented was that stuff didn't get processed through his head through some pre-conception of what it was supposed to be.'

In the Phoenix camp, River's lack of education is still seen as some kind of vindication of a natural, non-materialistic life-style. 'Our kids were so natural with everyone, so mature,' claims Arlyn. But who was this 'everyone'? Fellow child actors? Film technicians? Studio spin doctors? For River it was just something else to set him apart. Without the cut and thrust of the classroom, with its intense friendships and rivalries,

River Phoenix had no testing ground for peer relationships in the real world. It would serve him ill.

When River first arrived in Hollywood, he did go to school for a short time but he found it very unsettling. Already he lacked the social skills necessary to survive. Rather than persevering, John and Arlyn simply withdrew him, and from then on his education consisted of a series of statutory tutors which, according to Meredith Salenger, River's co-star on *Jimmy Reardon*, achieved nothing: 'When you're under eighteen you have to have three hours of school every day, so we would tell the social worker on the set that we were going to school, and then we'd go into River's trailer and talk and play, and when she'd come in we'd pick up books and read.'

River Phoenix was set apart from his peers in other ways too, as Joe Dante, director of *Explorers*, remembered. In this his first movie River was one of four child actors. He could have been one among equals. Yet Dante explains how River's sense of being an outsider was magnified by his strict dietary regime: 'Everything had to be done special for him. He had to have a special lunch; his parents wouldn't let him wear leather and stuff. He had to constantly explain that to people and justify it. River, I think, of all the kids, wanted to grow up fast. He didn't like the idea of being a kid.' He didn't like it because he had no experience of it in real life.

Already River's views on the environment were being eagerly sought by journalists hungry for a new take on the mini-hunk with a conscience. Yet the teen sage knew nothing. His goals were not self-developed, but hand-me-downs from his parents, in turn sentimental rather than informed. He had no background knowledge at all. But he was bright and had an appetite to learn. An appetite for knowledge and ordinary experience that, untutored and undirected, would prove self-destructive.

From early on River always felt more comfortable with older people. The lesson he

had learnt at his mother's knee was that there was nothing he could not do: he was the eco-prophet, saviour of the rain-forest, the creator of the Universe's own chosen one. Martha Plimpton recalled: 'He felt he was invincible.' And Judy Davis, co-star of his last, unfinished movie *Dark Blood* later recalled, 'He felt he was immune.'

According to Naomi Foner, River Phoenix could read and write, but that was it. His knowledge of literature, or history, was non-existent. Before he worked with Peter Bogdanovich on *The Thing Called Love* (1993), River had never heard of this famous director, let alone seen any of his films. He had never seen a James Dean film or an Orson Welles film. Dermot Mulrony, co-star on *The Thing Called Love* and Sam Shepard's *Silent Tongue*, found River's naivety unnerving. It was more than the 'don't know, don't care' of any other street-dumb teen rebel. 'He had no concept of Sam as a playwright or a screenwriter or a director or anything other than a sort of actor or well-known something or other. I had to explain to him what a Pulitzer prize was and what Sam won it for and why. He was under-educated and over-intelligent. In my opinion, Sam was completely and utterly perplexed by River. He was truly taken with him but couldn't figure him out. Sam would always have that crooked smile, watching, trying to figure out how much of this was River preparing to play an uncultured mad dog, and how much of it was really River.'

' I did get the sense that he was searching
and confused about things, and insecure.
He didn't have a lot of technique – you just
saw this kind of raw naturalism. You just
turned the camera on, and he would tell
the truth. '

Rob Reiner
Director, Stand By Me

Some 150 mourners gathered in the Paramount screening room for River Phoenix's
Hollywood memorial that afternoon of 25th November 1993. They were like disciples,
one observer said. The canonisation of River Phoenix had started as soon as news of his
death had hit the headlines, reinforced by the silence of family and friends. At the Cedars
Sinai Medical Centre where River had been taken – just two miles from The Viper Room
– River's ever-faithful agent Iris Burton and Sky Sworski took charge. No one was to talk.
Denial would be their common response. Arlyn took the first available flight from
Florida. John (with Summer, who had taken the phone call that gave them the news)
flew in from Costa Rica but by the time the Los Angeles police department had
instigated an enquiry about what had happened that night at The Viper Room, the family
had disappeared back to Florida. Their grief gave them free passage. Nothing would be
said.

In the days following his death the pavement outside The Viper Room was a shrine.
Chrysanthemums, tulips, roses and carnations. And candles guttering in the autumn
breeze. Chalked on the paving slabs in blue and gold was 'The Eternal River'. Federico
Fellini had died the same day but when it came to press coverage in Hollywood there
was no competition. Fellini after all was just a foreign film maker. And he died of old age.
But the 'live hard, die young' formula for immortality was all part of the Hollywood
myth, a trajectory that took in Marilyn Monroe, James Dean and John Belushi, who died
in March 1982 of a drug overdose at the Chateau Marmont, also on Sunset, just a block
down from The Viper Room.

Many of River's former professional associates gathered to remember the young man
they thought they had known so well. It was the third and last ceremony. Following the
Coroner's Inquest ('The manner of death is ruled as accidental'), River's body had been
returned to Florida where it was cremated, witnessed by sixty guests who paid their

farewells over the open-topped blue coffin where River lay dressed in his Aleka's Attic blue T-shirt, draped in beads, with a hank of hair cut for *Dark Blood* lying in a pony tail at the side. But not before photographs of River in the open coffin had been published by *The National Enquirer* who had paid a rumoured $5,000 for a snatched snap at the Milam Funeral Home.

The format for the third Hollywood Memorial Service remained the same as that of the first Memorial Service three weeks earlier, where there had been a large outdoor gathering in the grounds of the family's Micanopy property. An emotional address from Arlyn, followed by spontaneous testimonials from among the 150 mourners, among them Flea, Michael Stipe of REM and Dan Akroyd. The response of the Phoenix family and the 'Kling-ons' – the many hangers-on his money had supported – also remained in the same vein: variations on a general theme of 'River's in heaven. River was too good for this world. River needed to go, he's free now.'

But there were some who felt a real unease. Martha Plimpton, River's first and longest lasting girlfriend, was deeply angry. 'You would have thought he was ninety and had died in his sleep. The people who were saying this felt tremendous guilt that they had contributed to his death. He's already being made into a martyr. He's become a metaphor for a fallen angel, a Messiah. But he wasn't . He was just a boy, a very good-hearted boy who was very fucked-up and had no idea how to implement his good intentions. I don't want to be comforted by his death. I think it's right that I'm angry about it, angry at the people who helped him stay sick, and angry at River.'

As at his birth, so at his death, Arlyn was once more centre stage. Her hopes for her son, she said, had always been on a different plane to other stage mothers. And indeed that was true. The ambitions of most stage mothers extended at their most exalted to an Oscar. For Arlyn Phoenix, films were only the means to the end: 'We believed we could

use the mass media to help change the world and that River would be our missionary.'

A mother in grief should perhaps be granted the benefit of the doubt. But Martha Plimpton, who had known River longer and more intimately than anyone outside his family and was only too aware of the pressures he had faced, found Arlyn's new role as Mary-at-the-foot-of-the-Cross a cruel mockery.

'They created this Utopian bubble,' she said, 'so that River was never socialised – he was never prepared for dealing with crowds and with Hollywood, for the world in which he'd have to deliver the message. And furthermore when you're fifteen, to have to think of yourself as a prophet is unfair. His parents saw him as their saviour.'

By the time of the Hollywood memorial, River had been dead four weeks. The speculation of the first few days had been proved correct. The Coroner's report had showed that River Phoenix died of a lethal cocktail of drugs. The autopsy, which included a pharmacological screening of his body fluids, had revealed 'acute multiple drug intoxication ... lethal levels of cocaine and morphine'. The morphine was metabolized heroin at four times the lethal dose. The cocaine present was eight times the lethal dose. There was no evidence of needle marks. There was no evidence of alcohol. The feeling among the many professionals who had worked with River Phoenix over the years and who thought that they knew him was of stunned disbelief. At the Hollywood Memorial, after a series of emotional tributes and affecting anecdotes in which speakers hoped to draw from River Phoenix's life and death some kind of moral comfort, it took John Boorman, the English Director of *Deliverance*, to frame the question which no one else had dared to ask. 'Is there anybody here who can tell us why River took all those drugs?'

At this River's young sisters Liberty and Summer ran out of the screening room. The boy in the crowd had spoken. The young Emperor had no clothes.

THE RIVER PHOENIX ALBUM

At the time of his death, River Phoenix had completed thirteen feature films and was four-fifths through his last, *Dark Blood*. When a screen icon dies in such tragic circumstances it is tempting to imbue every last frame with genius. It was not so. But in *Stand By Me*, *The Mosquito Coast*, *Running On Empty*, *Dogfight* and *My Own Private Idaho*, River Phoenix gave performances of an exceptional quality and depth that marked him out as an actor for whom anything was possible.

The parallels between River's life and the characters he played were clear enough when he was alive. Watching his films now, with the knowledge of his death, adds yet another dimension to his already multi-layered performances.

Stand By Me, the film that made him, and arguably the film his performance made, opens with a newspaper headline: 'Attorney Chris Chambers fatally stabbed in Restaurant.' Although Chris Chambers, the moral heart and strength of the story, had succeeded in crossing the tracks and making it to college and beyond, his life was ultimately the stuff of tragedy. As was that of the young actor who so poignantly brought him to life on screen. Death by itself is not tragic. A tragedy is a death that could have been avoided. As co-star Gordie Lachance says at the close of the film: 'Although I hadn't seen him for ten years, I know I'll miss him forever.'

In mainstream films River continued to be cast to type. In both the black comedy *I Love You To Death* (1990) and in *Sneakers* (1992) he played variations on the theme of lovable misfit. Once again, in *Sneakers* the relationship with his father (Robert Redford) is the pivot that gives strength to an otherwise pretty run-of-the-mill caper movie. Working with high profile, experienced professionals like Robert Redford (*Sneakers*) and Kevin Kline (*I Love You To Death*) can be nerve-wracking from a personal stand-point for a young actor, but for River both proved fun rather than challenging. However, increasingly another River was beginning to emerge: the risk-taker, both in performance

and in his willingness to take his chances on box-office uncertainties. From now on there would be no more playing to teen-dream type. His trade-mark flyaway hair would be shorn (*Dogfight*, 1991) and dyed (*Dark Blood*). Even his sexual orientation would be put on the line (*My Own Private Idaho*). Such actors are rare.

For most actors acting is an exercise in illusion. But it was as if River Phoenix leased himself out to his character for the duration of the shooting schedule – and sometimes beyond – pitching himself into unknown territory on an imaginative journey whose end could never be second guessed. River's acceptance of the role of Birdlace, the young rookie marine in *Dogfight* was brave. This was a character he could feel no personal commitment to: 'There are things in the film that Birdlace does that if it were me, I'd be so embarrassed. But it's not me, it completely belongs to him.' The silky locks of the tousled-haired teen dream were discarded and River and all the other actor-marines were put through a five-day military 'boot camp' training. By the end, according to his co-star Anthony Clark, the metamorphosis was complete. 'On the first night we're out of boot camp, we went to this party, and it ended up that the police were called. All of us were onstage making rude gestures, and some of the guys were projectile vomiting off the stage. River was the head of that whole thing. I hate to talk bad about him but he had a mean streak. He wanted to get into a fight. That night he was a marine.'

Bobby Bukowski, director of photography on *Dogfight* described how River almost recklessly 'invited demons of the role into himself'. And those demons were not easily dislodged. 'After *Dogfight* I remember thinking he was being a real asshole – it took a month for him to become sweet again. And the street-urchin character in *Idaho* stayed with him and played into the whole drug thing.'

My Own Private Idaho is generally accepted to be River Phoenix's finest work. His portrayal of a narcoleptic rent boy is utterly compelling. There are few people who

could naturally identify with the character of Mike Waters, and yet in some extraordinary way through River's vulnerable yet wholly unsentimental performance we do. Although male homosexuality provides both the framework and the sub-text to the film, River is never limiting. Male, female, gay or straight, no one is excluded from the egg-shell fragility of his performance. The high profile casting of River with Keanu Reeves masks its art house origins. But for both actors it was a challenge worth taking.

True to form, River Phoenix went as far as he could in terms of research and preparation including, he claimed, being given oral sex by another male actor to find out what it was like because he knew that *My Own Private Idaho* would start with just such a controversial scene. Like any art house/low budget film, money was tight and hours were long. Unconventionally in Hollywood terms, River and eight other cast and crew members, (including Keanu Reeves), lived together in the director Gus van Sant's sprawling old house in Portland, Oregon, mirroring in many ways the communal life of the street kids in the film: working, eating, sleeping, playing music.

River totally immersed himself in the role, hanging out in Portland's seedy gay club, Vaseline Alley, walking Portland's meanstreets from two till six in the morning, hanging out with street hustlers, learning their body language, even pitching for 'dates'. But Mike Parker, a former runaway, River's guide to Portland's low life and source for his character, said that what most seemed to interest River was 'the brotherhood of the kids out here, how we were looking for acceptance and some man to be close to, looking for family'. For Eric Alan Edwards, director of photography, River's success was total. 'He looked like a street kid. In a very raw way he wore that role. I've never seen anybody so intent on living his role.' And that role included drugs.

William Richert, who had directed River in *Jimmy Reardon*, now found himself acting alongside the younger star, and saw the beginnings of River's drug use for himself:

'Some of those guys have been through it before and, when filming was finished, they gave it up and got back to their work. This was the time for River, though, and he went wild. He wasn't mature enough to leave it and go back to his clean life.'

Corey Feldman, co-star in *Stand By Me*, who developed a serious drug problem towards the end of the eighties, said he had heard that River was doing heroin. As a previous user himself (though by then clean) he recognised the signs. 'Watching clips from the film and looking at the pictures and interviews with him, and the way he was talking and the way he was acting, I presumed it to be true.' Corey Feldman decided to try and help his friend. But it was not to be. 'He was in a lot of denial and said 'I'm fine, everything's fine.' That kind of thing.'

The split between reality and myth was growing wider. In public, River Phoenix continued to denounce all forms of drug-taking. 'They're a short cut to an altered state. I don't see any point or any good in drugs that are as disruptive as cocaine. I never tried heroin. I tried alcohol and most of the others when I was fifteen and got it out of the way – finished with that stuff.' But the clues were there if you wanted to hear them: 'You don't have to seek it out, it finds you. In the dressing room or the make-up trailer, someone will say, "If you don't tell anyone, I'll let you try some." It's so accessible and so stylish. I hate all that.' But nobody chose to hear.

My Own Private Idaho was the watershed. Before then River had been an occasional, recreational user. Now, although sporadic, drug taking was part of what he did. Who he was. For Martha Plimpton it was enough to break up their three-and-a-half year relationship which had started on *The Mosquito Coast*. 'He really liked getting drunk and high but he didn't have a gauge when to stop. When we split up, a lot of it was that I had learned that screaming, fighting and begging wasn't going to change him, that he had to change himself, and that he didn't want to yet.' But their friendship continued.

According to her, his drug use came in spurts. 'He'd often be very high when he called. His language would become totally incoherent.'

For any celebrity user, taking drugs is laced with elaborate games of deceit. Friends and colleagues have to be carefully screened. Different people have different access. There are friends who know nothing. Friends who you smoke with, friends you do coke with, people you freebase with, people you leave behind when you go to the bathroom.

The split between the two Rivers, the drug-taking partying loud-mouth, and the introverted tofu-eating lover of rain forests was a stark manifestation of his desperate internal struggle to find himself. There were so many contradictions. He was a child star with the gravitas of a grandfather, yet as an adult man retained the looks and demeanour of a teenager. He was a sage who knew nothing. He was torn between adulation and obscurity, wealth and simplicity. It was an unwinnable race between the arrogant film star who got what he wanted and the abandoned boy, desperate for approval and love. River Phoenix was a mess and certainly by the time he was filming *The Thing Called Love*, he knew it: 'I'm being jerked around in the way you're always jerked around. They want you to do what they want you to do. I have twenty personalities on top of the ten I already have. So now I have thirty people in my head.'

Each of these thirty had a different tale to tell. For River Phoenix there was no division between acting or being. Ten days before his death he told a French reporter, 'I have lied and changed stories and contradicted myself left and right, so that at the end of the year you could read five different articles and say, "This guy is schizophrenic".' This was nothing new. Three years before on *Little Nikita* he was already confused: 'Whenever people tell me to be myself, I don't know what to do. I don't know what myself is' But the drugs made it worse.

Recreational drugs may be tolerated in the film industry, but in the music industry

they're endemic. Increasingly, River found himself drawn into his musician friends' world: their company and their clubs. River had sung and played the guitar since he was six. Music was what had got him into Hollywood and music remained his first love. In Florida he put together a band, called Aleka's Attic. Playing in the local music spot, The Hardback Cafe, River could be, as near as was possible, incognito, just another musician. But any equality he imagined between himself and the members of the band was illusory. They were all beholden to him. Just like the 'Kling-ons'. The family house at Micanopy was home to around twelve of the 'tofu mafia' as they were known to River's more self-sufficient friends. They lived and worked on the property, in caravans dotted around the place and even in River's own apartment above his recording studio.

Rachel Guinan, a single parent with money worries following a car accident, worked as a barmaid at The Hardback Cafe. She was deeply touched when Aleka's Attic did a benefit for her. But she took the decision not to get involved either with River personally, or his entourage. 'They were a bunch of vultures feeding off River and I didn't want to be one of them.' She had met him off and on over the years: 'He was an innocent sweet boy at first but I saw him become more arrogant and callous as time went on. At first he was very open, natural, earnest. But he trusted too many people, and it killed him.' Her view of Arlyn is hardly more charitable: 'She's got them under her thumb. She made all the decisions about money. I can't help but feel resentment because they were all so much more on top of things than River was.'

Sky Sworski was another hometown friend who had known River since he first arrived in Florida, aged seven, and on the Phoenix's return to Gainesville became one of the inner circle, older than River, younger than his parents. 'He definitely changed. When you're around Hollywood people and the money and everything, you change. But it took a long time. I guess by the time he turned nineteen, he had a band and he wanted

to be a little bit of a kid. And he was. They used to play in this huge attic above the band room. Sometimes we went out on tour. The only time we'd use his name was if we did a benefit concert for, like, the rain forest or indigenous people or cancer or Bill Clinton. He wanted to hang out with his peers, because he was usually hanging out with these movie set people who were older. He was always hanging out with older people.' But Sky didn't know about the drugs. 'He kept it from me. Because there would have been trouble.'

There were few people brave enough to face River with the truth of where he was heading. One was Bobby Bukowski, another was Dirk Drake, who had been tutor to all the Phoenix children, including River, and who was still the history teacher at Westwood, the local school outside Gainesville, Florida. In December 1991 Drake and River had a show-down. It happened in Los Angeles, in a rented house belonging to Flea (Michael Balzary), bassist with The Red Hot Chilli Peppers, who River considered his closest friend. He had grown close to Flea while filming *My Own Private Idaho* in which the musician played the peroxide punk Budd. The house was shared by other friends of Flea's and, on this occasion, according to Drake, one of these 'drug crazed' young men had run amok in a jealous rage and chased River around the house with a butcher's knife. 'Don't worry,' River told Drake, 'I have the fear of God. I want to live to see what the higher power's purpose is for me.'

The most important person who claimed not to know about the drugs was Arlyn, his mother. Bobby Bokowski was amazed by her blinkered view of her son: 'You'd have to be really dumb or naive not to know he was high when he was. He was clearly so high, he was like an alien.'

After his death, Arlyn was finally forced to concede that River's life wasn't as perfect as the version the myth had presented. 'As River grew he did become more and more

uncomfortable being the poster boy for all good things. He often said he wished he could just be anonymous. But he never was. When he wasn't a movie star, he was a missionary. There's a beauty in that – the man with the cause, the leader – but there's also a deep loneliness.'

After his death the worms began to turn. There were interviews with fellow actors, musicians, junkies, pushers. All of whom were now happy to add their reminiscences to the late River Phoenix tragedy file. Yes, they'd snorted cocaine/heroin with him. Yes, they'd done speedballs together. And of course the new designer drug GHB. One claimed he'd taught him to shoot up. How much was true, how much uncheckable invention just to hitch a ride on the publicity hearse, is impossible to judge.

Jim Barton, writer of *Dark Blood* believes everyone knew the trouble River was in. 'It was obvious. You only had to have a conversation with him to know he was stoned. But this is Hollywood and people are sold according to their image and River's image was squeaky clean. No one was prepared to rock that boat. To an astonishing degree. To the point where when the paramedics arrive, right to the moment when he's on the sidewalk, when he's moments from death... These paramedics carry an antidote for heroin overdose. They didn't use it because all they were told was that he had taken some Valium. And they're still living this lie because it's the ticket.'

According to Barton, at the end of 1994 a friend of River's had spoken out on television and told how he had tried to get River into drug rehabilitation a year before he died. But the offer was refused. 'If he had a drug problem it was completely unacceptable to admit to anybody that he had, because it went against his image and that's how everyone was making their money.'

George Sluizer, director of *Dark Blood*, remembers standing in a hotel corridor in Utah listening to Arlyn telling him how 'clean' River was, while at the same time he

could smell the marijuana drifting down the corridor from River's room even as they were talking.

Like Martha Plimpton, ('I don't want to be comforted by his death... I'm angry at the people who helped him stay sick'), Jim Barton is not afraid to point the finger. 'The nicest thing you could say,' says Barton, 'is that they all turned a blind eye. For everyone – from agents, family, the entourage – River was the meal ticket.'

There is never a shortage of people who want to hang out with a star. On what would be the last night of his life River Phoenix had the weekend off from filming in Utah and was ready to party. Shooting on *Dark Blood* was tough. The locations were dangerous. It was a tense set: River and the director George Sluizer were often at loggerheads and it was a far cry from the haven described by Arlyn in a letter to the *Los Angeles Times* on 24th November: 'He had just arrived in LA from the pristine beauty and quietness of Utah..... We felt that the excitement and energy of the Hallowe'en nightclub and art scene were beyond his usual experience and control.'

River was booked into the Nikki, a new Japanese business Hotel on La Cienaga Boulevard. When in Hollywood he usually stayed at the St James Club, a converted 1930s apartment block. The Nikki Hotel wasn't used to hell-raising VIPs and when Room Service returned from delivering drinks and food, they reported that the suite was in chaos and that the young star was out of his head. When River ordered his car to be brought around at 10.30, he and his entourage were already the worse for wear and made a rumpus in the marble-clad lobby, with its tinkling post-modernist waterfall. The next day cocaine and heroin were found in his rooms.

The Viper Room was on the corner of Larabee and Sunset, only a couple of blocks away from La Cienaga. It was West Hollywood's newest, hippest nite spot and had been

opened that August. It was co-owned by the young film star Johnny Depp who, like River, was into music. The last three years had seen a resurgence in the club scene in West Hollywood as the police department had relaxed the clean-up campaign which got into gear following John Belushi's death. Each club had its own particular identity, based on music, dress code and age. The Viper Room was pitched at the 'young music crowd', rather than the glitzy Tatou or the Roxbury, frequented by Armani-clad Eurotrash. The Viper Room had been designed to look like a vintage Hollywood speakeasy. Behind the corner bandstand was a tropical island mural. Around the back wall of the club were a series of booths with 'private' tables, lit by green art deco lights. It could hold up to 200 people and unlike The Whisky across the street was a place primarily for dancing and music; live music. The Red Hot Chilli Peppers were playing that night but things were very relaxed. It was a hang out for musicians who would take the opportunity to jam with whoever was around. That night, all being well, River would join them on stage.

To get into The Viper Room you had to be 21. But it catered for the younger crowd and fake IDs were always to be had from the hustlers prowling the Strip. On the night of the 30/31 October 1993, the joint was pulsing.

Somebody else drove River's car the few hundred yards from the hotel. He was slumped in the back. Inside the club he was joined by his brother Leaf, sister Rain and Samantha Mathis, his current girlfriend and co-star on *The Thing Called Love*. They had a table in one of the booths. It was Saturday night and an anonymous actress remembers how crowded it was. She first knew something was wrong when she saw her friend Samantha 'freaking out' and tried to calm her down. 'River was barely able to stand. He kept leaping up and bumping into things, his words were so slurred you could barely understand him.'

The Viper Room boasts a celebrities-only VIP lounge. That night it was full. There are

conflicting accounts of what actually happened. Who River met. What he took. But all agree that just before midnight after he returned to the table he began vomiting over himself. Friends, members of the entourage, took him to the men's room to clean up. They splashed cold water on his face then got him back to the table. At this point the seizures began. He slumped down and slid under the table. He said he couldn't breathe. Said he needed air. Leaf and Samantha took hold of the thin, strung out anonymous figure in black jeans and Converse sneakers and made for the easiest exit, the stage door behind the bandstand. The Red Hot Chilli Peppers were playing and Johnny Depp was jamming with them. As Leaf and Samantha dragged him past the stage he called out: 'Hey Dude, I've done a speedball. I'm going to die.'

Johnny Depp didn't stop playing. He hadn't recognised the white-faced, brown-haired boy they were carrying out.

FADE OUT

ROLL CREDITS

'I think River was like my late son. He was years ahead of his age. I think people like that are very vulnerable to. . . well, to other people. They are prey for the not-so-good.'
Alan Bates
Co-star, Silent Tongue

'They came to me when they were little children, the whole family. I've had them since River was, like, nine. He was the most beautiful child you've ever seen, like a little Elvis.'
Iris Burton
River Phoenix's agent

'He often said he wished he could just be anonymous, but he never was. When he wasn't a movie star, he was a missionary.'
Arlyn Phoenix

'He bought up acres and acres of forests. He did not invest in condos; he bought rain forests. He spent thousands and thousands of dollars, just so they wouldn't be cut down. That's what he was doing with his money.'
William Richert
Director, Jimmy Reardon

'I feel really bad, because I felt like he was there for everybody, and nobody was there for him. I knew maybe there were problems. . . .but he was such a great actor that he would just totally calm my nerves. I mean, he would make you feel crazy for even asking him, "Is everything all right?"'
Anthony Clark
Co-star Dogfight, The Thing Called Love

'One time we were up in the mountains, and the clouds came right up to the top of the mountain. River grabbed (my) arm and said, "We're going to run and jump into these clouds and our whole past lives will dissolve, and everything will be new from then on. Hold on." And we did that. . . it was incredible, and we landed on this soft iceberg kind of ground covering. But we jumped through clouds, literally.'
William Richert
Director, Jimmy Reardon

'There was always an outsider quality to him. I think he must have felt that way somewhat, because his family was unusual and his name was unusual.'
Joe Dante
Director, Explorers

'He sent a very sweet letter and a present after Larry [Olivier, her husband] died. It was a tuning fork, and the message said, "Tune in to life."'
Joan Plowright
Co-star, I Love You To Death

'We talked the entire day. One of the reasons I opened up to him is that I felt he did understand and felt how I did – not the same way, but the pain.'
Michael Parker
Inspiration for River's character in Idaho

'River Phoenix was a victim of the machine. The fame machine, the Hollywood machine, the selling machine, the money machine. And the machine is a liar.'
Jim Barton
Screenwriter, Dark Blood

'I know one thing: River did not want to die. He had too much going on. . .But I guess that's part of what happens. . . it's a release. People find different ways of escaping. He had a lot of stress, not only on the set.'
Sky Sworski
Friend and benefactor

'We did ten takes of the soliloquy, the last day we shot with him on *Dark Blood*. It was in the cave. . . all lit by candles. After the last take I didn't turn off the camera. When we saw the dailies, for ten seconds River was in front of the camera, just a silhouette lit by ambient light. It was. . . .eerie. People were crying. We knew that was the last we would see of River.'
Ed Lachman
Director of photography, Dark Blood